INFANTRY OF THE FUTURE

Roderic D. Schmidt

The Rosen Publishing Group, Inc., New York

For Katie

Published in 2006 by The Rosen Publishing Group, Inc.
29 East 21st Street, New York, NY 10010

First Edition

Library of Congress Cataloging-in-Publication Data

Schmidt, Roderic D.
Infantry of the future / Roderic D. Schmidt.—1st ed.
    p. cm.—(The library of future weaponry)
Includes bibliographical references and index.
ISBN 1-4042-0525-X (library binding)
1. Field service (Military science)—Juvenile literature. 2. Infantry—Juvenile literature.
3. Military weapons—Juvenile literature. I. Title. II. Series.
UD145.S36 2006
356'.1—dc22
                                                                    2005015322

Manufactured in the United States of America

On the cover: Soldiers are armed and ready for combat in this image from a poster announcing the U.S. Army's Future Combat Systems.

CONTENTS

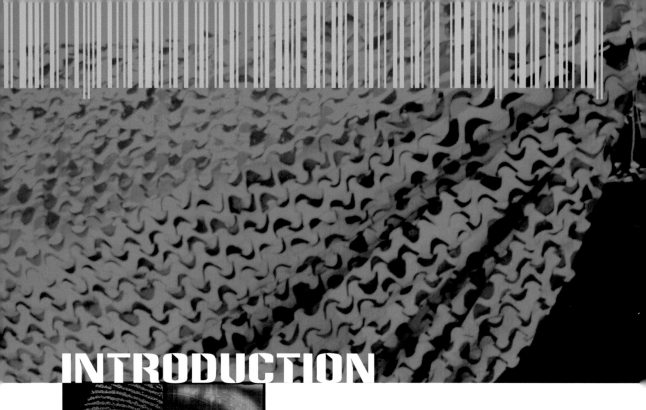

INTRODUCTION

The infantry consists of soldiers who are trained, armed, and equipped to fight on foot. The infantry has long been the most important part of a nation's armed forces. However, it has also been the least glamorous unit. The word "infantry" is derived from the Latin word for "child." This is because the foot soldier was seen as having a childlike inability to make decisions. For centuries, members of the infantry were trained just enough to function on the battlefield and obey orders from powerful and intimidating commanders.

In the past fifty years, the role of the infantry has changed dramatically. Infantry missions are more varied and complex than ever before. Peacekeeping and police force missions, where communication skills are more important than brute force, have become more common. The fighting of nonnational armed forces, such as terrorists, has also become a major responsibility of the infantry today.

The changing nature of warfare requires that the infantry receives more sophisticated training than in the past. This advanced training is important because today's foot soldier is under much more pressure to perform than ever before. If a soldier accidentally kills a civilian, it will be reported by the media all over the world. One soldier's actions may affect world politics. The infantry of today and tomorrow must be lethal in combat but also wise in judgment. It is a job for dedicated, well-trained, and well-equipped professionals.

This book will discuss the United States' infantry of the future—its weapons, training, and possible missions. This future will be marked by a shift away from conventional, high-intensity warfare against similarly equipped foes. Instead, the infantry of the future will consist of lighter, more mobile forces. The soldiers of the infantry will be highly trained and able to adapt to many different battle situations.

TRAINING TOMORROW'S INFANTRY

Many people believe technology is the most important factor in determining the strength of a nation's army. This is unfortunate because it has caused many militaries to focus on high-tech "wonder weapons" instead of concentrating on the training of their soldiers.

The importance of training is illustrated by the Battle of Mogadishu in Somalia in 1993. In this battle, a few dozen U.S. Army Rangers and Delta Force troops fought their way past thousands of Somali fighters. The U.S. troops had Humvees and a technological advantage with their body armor, but the Somalis had more men and the advantage of operating in familiar territory. The fact that the battle was fought in a city also favored the Somalis. The tall buildings and other urban structures affected U.S. communications systems, provided hiding places for the enemy, and made it

Specialized training prepares tomorrow's soldier for battle in urban areas. This photograph from 2004 shows soldiers of a Stryker brigade combat team searching a city street for enemy combatants as part of Operation Iraqi Freedom. Among the many unique challenges of urban warfare is being able to identify an enemy who has blended in with the larger civilian population.

difficult for the United States to use their long-range firepower. It was the U.S. soldiers' superior training that allowed them to fight their way out. They lost 18 men, and 500 to 1,000 Somalis died. A unit with less training probably would have been completely wiped out.

BASIC TRAINING

Currently, training for an infantryman in the U.S. Army is fourteen to sixteen weeks, depending on the soldier's specialization. U.S.

WOMEN IN THE INFANTRY

This book uses only masculine pronouns (he, him, or his) when referring to U.S. infantry. This is because according to Army Regulation 600-13 women are not allowed to join "units which are assigned a routine mission to engage in direct combat, or which collocate [are located near] routinely with units assigned a direct combat mission." This means that women in the U.S. Army cannot serve in the infantry. Other branches of the U.S. military, except the Coast Guard, also have restrictions preventing women from serving in certain jobs. These restrictions are mostly because of tradition and are not because women are believed to be incapable of fighting on the modern and future battlefield.

Marines train for nineteen to twenty-three weeks. Initial combat training for army and marine recruits is unlikely to change very much in the future. Classroom work combined with field and live-fire exercises will continue to prepare troops for the sights, sounds, and smells of the battlefield.

While the initial training of the infantry will remain the same, later training and coursework will be different. Approximately 13 percent of marines are in training at any given time, taking them away from their units and back to training camp. The marines and the army have a plan to begin offering many classes online. This will allow soldiers to take classes while deployed with their units. The U.S. military's commitments across the globe seem likely to increase in the coming years and will spread its manpower ever thinner. Because of this, online training is a trend that will likely continue to grow.

TRAINING WITH SIMULATORS

Another likely change in the training of infantry will be the increased use of simulators. Basically, these are electronic games that put the player in real-world situations. They have been used for vehicle and aircraft crew members for a few years now, and they are increasingly being developed for the infantry. *Full Spectrum Warrior* is a simulator that the army developed with Pandemic Studios and is already in use. The army has also created a video game called *America's Army* in which the player participates in realistic training drills.

Many of the simulators have devices to shake, shock, and startle players when they are wounded or killed in the game. These simulators will provide valuable experience and reaction-time training for soldiers. They create situations in which a soldier's actions have measurable consequences, but put him in no real danger. Equipment and ammunition expenses will also be reduced by the use of simulators.

As virtual reality technologies become more sophisticated, military simulators will follow suit. The more real a simulator can be made to feel for a player, the more useful it will be. The sounds and sights of the battlefield are the emphasis in today's

Simulators are increasingly being used to train the infantry. *America's Army* is a simulator created by the army that can be downloaded for free from its Web site. In this photograph, a designer of *America's Army* uses a machine gun to destroy a virtual enemy at Camp Guernsey, an army training center in Wyoming that specializes in battlefield simulation.

simulators. Those two senses will continue to be the focus of simulation design in the future. Improvements in computer power and audio-visual technology will make these simulations more and more difficult to tell apart from reality. Smell and temperature sensation may also be added, further increasing the realistic qualities of the training.

SPECIALTY TRAINING

There will be three areas of concentration for the training of U.S. infantrymen in the future. The first, Military Operations in Urban Terrain (MOUT), will become increasingly important as the foes of the United States continue to draw U.S. forces into urban areas. Peacekeeping and policing missions will also increase and will require additional specialized training. Terrorist organizations prosper in unstable and failed states, and American forces are likely to be deployed to help stabilize nations on the brink of collapse. Finally, more highly trained special forces, such as the Army Rangers, Delta Force, and Navy SEALs are likely to be needed for hostage rescue and other complex missions. These last forces are expensive to train and maintain, but they give the United States more options when unusual situations arise.

Military Operations in Urban Terrain

Over the years, it has become less likely that the United States will be involved in a war against conventional heavy (tank-using) forces. This became especially true after the first Gulf War in 1991. In this war, Saddam Hussein attempted to use his forces in a conventional manner in open country against the U.S. forces. The result was that the United States completely overwhelmed Hussein's forces.

The first Gulf War showed the world exactly how not to fight the United States. Any adversary who wants to engage the United States in the future is likely to try to bring the conflict into an urban area. The difficult terrain and presence of civilians in urban warfare negates the strengths of the U.S. forces. Buildings restrict fire and reduce the range of most engagements to the width of a street or smaller. Buildings also provide cover for the enemy and disrupt radio communications. The possibility of civilian casualties prevents commanders from using heavy support such as artillery and air strikes. Armored vehicles are vulnerable to attacks in cities and are rarely used there. All this makes MOUT a battle between men with little more than rifles and other small arms. In these situations, the quality of the infantry's training is often the difference between victory or defeat.

Peacekeeping and Policing

Peacekeeping and policing missions, while less dangerous, will also require intensive training. Like urban warfare, this type of mission is full of unique challenges. The man on the ground in these missions will not be able to use force in many situations, since the local population is not regarded as an enemy. There may be civilians hostile to U.S. forces. Soldiers may have to separate groups while remaining neutral and refraining from combat. There may also be a language barrier with the local population. An infantryman on such a mission needs to combine the threat of force with the skills of a counselor to keep tense situations from becoming deadly.

Special Forces

The Department of Defense is planning on increasing the number of Special Forces troops as well. These highly trained soldiers proved vital in ousting the Taliban from Afghanistan without the need for a large U.S. presence on the ground. They

U.S. Marines and Canadian soldiers patrol a neighborhood in Port-au-Prince, Haiti, on June 17, 2004. International peacekeeping forces have been stationed in Haiti for a number of years in order to help prevent outbreaks of violence while the country puts together a new government. Infantry will continue to be involved in similar peacekeeping operations in the future.

are also of use in capturing enemy leaders and in raiding enemy camps. Hostage rescue is another critical mission they undertake. As the world changes, the hard-hitting, precision strike options that the Special Forces give the United States will become more and more important.

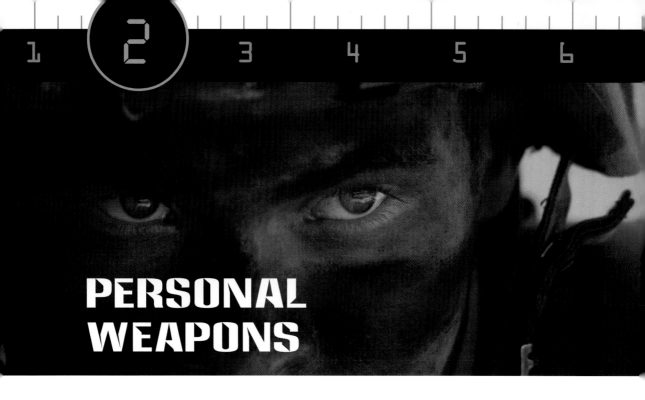

PERSONAL WEAPONS

The personal weapons of the infantry are the main tools for nearly all military operations. The man on the ground with his rifle, machine gun, and grenade occupies territory and represents the power of his nation. Warplanes, armored vehicles, artillery, warships, and other technological devices get the infantryman where he needs to go and help him do his job.

The U.S. Army is in the midst of developing a new crop of small arms and equipment that will make the American foot soldier ten times more deadly and ten times better protected than he is now. This new set of weapons is expected to be in use by 2020.

THE CURRENT STATE OF WEAPONRY

The current weapons found in an infantry platoon are diverse and deadly. The standard assault rifle is the M-16A3. This rifle began service in a slightly different version in the 1960s. Some of the older versions and variants are still in service. The M-16A3 fires 5.56 mm bullets. It weighs about 7 pounds (3.2 kilograms) and is very accurate to a quarter of a mile (400 meters).

The M-4 is a lighter and shorter carbine version of the M-16A3. It is used by most regular infantry troops as well as Special Forces troops. It is especially effective for use in close quarters. For more sustained firepower, troops carry the extremely reliable M-249 squad automatic weapon. This weapon weighs 22 pounds (10 kg). It fires the 5.56 mm rounds as well, but uses 200-round belts of ammunition, allowing it to keep up a deadly rate of fire.

Troops also have the M-203 40 mm grenade launcher, which attaches under the barrel of the M-16A3. It can fire grenades out to 500 feet (150 m). For close-range combat, the M-67 explosive hand grenade is used. The AN-M-14 incendiary hand grenade is used to melt holes in and fuse the metal parts of vehicles and machinery.

LAND WARRIOR

Land Warrior (LW) is a system that will combine new weapons, protective equipment and clothing, communications gear, and personal computers for army and marine infantry. Troops are already testing versions of Land Warrior gear. Full deployment should happen in the next few years.

In the short term, some of the first changes that the U.S. infantry will see are upgrades to the M-16 and M-4 rifles. The

A soldier models the Land Warrior system, which is currently being developed by the U.S. Army. The system consists of everything that an infantry soldier needs to wear or carry into battle. Components include body armor, a helmet, weapons, a personal computer, and communications equipment. Land Warrior will create a soldier who is better protected, deadlier, and more mobile than ever before.

Land Warrior system will add electrical parts to these rifles. A thermal weapon sight connected to a tiny eyepiece screen will enable troops to look and fire around cover while exposing only their hands. A laser range finder and digital compass will provide troops with precise range and direction information. The range finder and compass, together with global positioning system (GPS) technology, will enable soldiers to call in heavier fire from artillery and aircraft as needed.

XM-8 FUTURE COMBAT RIFLE

The XM-8 future combat rifle is likely to replace the M-16 and M-4. This weapon could start service as early as 2006. The

A soldier test fires an early prototype of the XM-8 future combat rifle. The XM-8 will likely replace the army's M-16 and M-4 rifles sometime in the near future. The XM-8 can be reconfigured into four different versions of the weapon. Pictured above is the standard carbine version.

XM-8 fires the same 5.56 mm ammunition as the M-16 and M-4. It uses 10-, 30-, or 100-round magazines that are clear so the operator can see how much ammunition he has left. It can fire in single shots, full automatic, and three-round burst modes. It weighs only 6.2 pounds (2.8 kg) and is mechanically very reliable. Much of the LW add-on parts for the M-16 and M-4 are standard features for the XM-8.

The XM-8 is 29.8 inches (0.76 m) long and can be used just as easily by both right- and left-handed soldiers. It can be customized into four different versions: a standard version for general use, a sharpshooter version for snipers, an ultracompact version for combat in close quarters, and an automatic rifle variant for more sustained fire. The automatic rifle variant will fulfill the same role that the M-249 currently has, but will have more interchangeable parts that can be used with the other weapons in a squad.

The XM-8 has a battery-powered sight that includes a red-dot laser for close-range targeting, an infrared laser for aiming in darkness and bad weather, and a laser illuminator for marking targets for laser-guided weapons.

XM-8 MODIFICATIONS

The XM-320 grenade launcher will replace the M-203. The XM-320 will mount under the barrel of the XM-8. It will fire 40 mm grenades and 25 mm grenades that are loaded one at a time from the side. The 40 mm grenades are the same as used by the M-203, but the 25 mm grenades are new. The 25 mm grenades have a range of more than half a mile (800 meters) and variable fuse settings. These settings allow a soldier to set the grenade to explode on impact or to burst in the air above a target. The 25 mm grenade even has a self-destruct function, so that if it misses its target, it will explode after eight seconds. This minimizes the unexploded grenades on the battlefield, which are a significant danger to civilians and soldiers of both sides.

The XM-8 operator can mount the LSS lightweight twelve-gauge shotgun underneath the barrel instead of the XM-320. The shotgun holds one shell at a time and can fire standard ammunition as well as nonlethal ammunition for crowd control and similar situations. It even has special breaching

Soldiers test the Land Warrior system at the U.S. Army Infantry Center in Fort Benning, Georgia. The soldier on the right is using his rifle to look around the corner without exposing any part of his body. This feature and others make the system an impressive combination of power and protection.

ammunition, which is used for shooting through the hinges and locks on doors when infantrymen are clearing out buildings.

M-240G

The M-60 medium machine gun has recently been replaced in the Marine Corps and the army with the M-240G. This machine gun, built by the Belgian company FN Herstal, has been in use in several other nations' armies since the 1960s. Its performance on paper is very similar to the M-60. However, it is much more reliable than the M-60, so it jams less and will function in more severe weather conditions. Even though the

A marine fires a M-240G medium machine gun in this photograph from May 7, 2005. The soldier was participating in a joint training exercise involving the armed forces of the United States, Japan, Thailand, Singapore, the Philippines, and Mongolia. The training, known as Exercise Cobra Gold, focused on preparing soldiers of these nations for future peacekeeping and humanitarian assistance missions.

weapon is already fifty years old, the M-240G provides everything the infantry of the future will need in a medium machine gun. Rather than reinvent the wheel, preexisting technology is being used instead. This allows the army to spend more on the development of other weapons.

PREDATOR SHORT-RANGE ASSAULT WEAPON

The army and Marine Corps are currently developing a cheap, single-use missile called the Predator short-range assault weapon (SRAW). This missile will be used in urban combat. It was in the field in an earlier model designed to destroy vehicles, but is now being redesigned as a bunker-busting weapon. The Predator SRAW is about 35 inches (0.9 m) long and only weighs about 20 pounds (9 kg). It is fired directly at a target within a quarter mile (400 m) and is unguided. It has a "soft-launch" capability, so it can be fired safely from within a bunker or building without the dangerous backblast associated with most missiles. Once completed, it will allow infantrymen to carry a little artillery wherever they may go.

EQUIPMENT

The personal weapons of the infantry are the most basic tools they need to do their job, but other nonweapon equipment is also of great importance. Some things, like body armor, have an obvious benefit. Other things may seem trivial but prove important in the field, such as a system of packs and straps for carrying gear and properly distributing the weight to reduce fatigue.

The Land Warrior system is currently being tested by limited numbers of U.S. soldiers. The system will be phased into the infantry over the next ten years. It will be used by all five kinds of infantry in the U.S. Army: ranger, airborne, air assault, light, and mechanized. The Marine Corps and air force are also interested in the program. The goal of the LW system is to combine small arms and high-tech equipment to allow U.S. infantry to win on any twenty-first–century battlefield.

LAND WARRIOR SUBSYSTEMS

Land Warrior consists of five major components, which can be customized to enhance an individual soldier's mission. The weapon subsystem was detailed in the previous chapter. The other four subsystems are the integrated helmet assembly, computer/radio, software, and protective clothing/individual equipment.

Integrated Helmet Assembly

Land Warrior's integrated helmet assembly subsystem is constructed of advanced lightweight material to increase protection and comfort. There is a small computer and sensor display, allowing soldiers to view maps, intelligence data, troop locations, and images captured with the thermal weapon sight.

Computer/Radio

The computer/radio subsystem (CRS) will attach to the backpack frame of the LW. It will consist of a computer, radio, and global positioning system in one unit. A hand grip on the soldier's chest will be attached to the CRS, providing control for the helmet-mounted display. The hand grip will also control the radio and allow the soldier to send digital information (such as video or photographs) to other soldiers or a command center.

The CRS has two versions: the standard one described above, and an advanced version for officers. The version for officers adds a second radio and a flat-panel display/keyboard. Improvements

The Interceptor body armor consists of a vest, protective inserts, and removable collar, throat, and groin protectors. All of the components together weigh 16 pounds (7.3 kg), which is nearly 10 pounds (4.5 kg) lighter than previously issued body armor. The body armor is already in use and has been credited with saving the lives of numerous U.S. soldiers during combat in Afghanistan and Iraq.

in computer processors are anticipated to reduce the size of the CRS panel to about the size of a credit card. The panel will be embedded in the fabric of the LW gear.

Software

The software subsystem contains programs to help analyze maps, intelligence, and mission data. The software system is designed to be upgradable, so future improvements can be installed. The software also has a power-management function to stretch the life of the LW batteries. The power system is currently a bit of a problem in the development of LW. Developers have found it difficult to make batteries that are small but powerful enough to keep the system running for a long time.

Protective Clothing/Individual Equipment

Land Warrior's protective clothing/individual equipment sub-system features a backpack frame that uses automotive racing technology to conform to the movement of a soldier's body. The frame adjusts to the soldier's load in order to minimize fatigue.

The Interceptor body armor continues the army's trend of greater protection with less weight. It is a modular system that can add on plates for use in heavier combat. These additional plates can stop small-arms fire from point-blank range. Interceptor armor has been used in the field already (without the rest of the LW system) and has been well received by the troops using it.

FUTURE FORCE WARRIOR

Future Force Warrior (FFW) is a system of equipment that will improve upon the Land Warrior system. Scheduled for deployment beginning in 2010, it will make infantry ten times more dangerous and protected.

The FFW armor will be lighter yet more protective than the Interceptor armor of the LW system. The hard part of the FFW armor will rest 2 to 3 inches (5 to 7.6 centimeters) away from the body, so the impact of bullets will be better distributed and less likely to harm the wearer. This is important because body armor will often stop a bullet but crack ribs or seriously bruise the soldier.

The communications system of FFW will be even more connected than that of Land Warrior. Soldiers will be able to share data with each other, and with nearby vehicles and aircraft.

An army colonel *(left)* examines a soldier modeling the Future Force Warrior equipment. As can be seen in this photo, the body armor of the Future Force Warrior rests slightly off the body in order to reduce the impact of a bullet or other projectile. Future Force Warrior will also include a body monitoring system that can transmit information about the soldier's health to a medical team.

The idea is to create a system in which information received by one soldier will become instantly available to everyone. FFW will have a personal radio allowing all members of a squad to keep in contact with each other. A helmet-mounted voice sensor will pick up vibrations from the soldier's head when he speaks. This will let soldiers talk to each other without the need for an obtrusive microphone.

The computer system of the FFW will be voice activated, and mission data will show up on a clear, eye-level screen. This heads-up display will let a soldier use his computer without taking his attention away from the battlefield. The computer will also be connected to sensors that will show the soldier's body core temperature, skin temperature, heart rate, water consumption, and whether the soldier is standing or sitting down. This data can be accessed by other soldiers to determine the health of their fellow soldiers. It will also allow medics miles away to monitor soldiers in extreme temperatures for heatstroke and hypothermia. The medic can then radio the soldier and instruct him how to treat the condition, or transmit a map to the soldier showing him the location of medical personnel.

The Future Force Warrior will use existing weapons at first, most likely the XM-8 rifle. Over time, the FFW will be equipped with a combined assault rifle/grenade launcher. This gun will likely look something like the XM-29 objective individual combat weapon. The XM-29 was an attempt at a combined weapon that has been put on hold until a few problems concerning its construction can be worked out.

VISION 2020 FUTURE FORCE WARRIOR

On the far horizon of infantry equipment is the Vision 2020 Future Force Warrior. This program is in the idea stage. It will incorporate a number of technologies that are only beginning to be developed. Land Warrior and Future Force Warrior are new systems, but soldiers using them still look like modern soldiers. The Vision 2020 FFW is radically different. The current designs

The Vision 2020 Future Force Warrior is the army's vision of how a soldier will be outfitted in the distant future. The system, including the headgear and uniform, will be tailored to each individual soldier. The system is in the earliest stages of development, and many technological hurdles must be overcome before it is ready for combat.

look like a cross between a motocross biker and a ninja.

The main thing that will make Vision 2020 FFW so different is nanotechnology. Nanotechnology involves the construction of materials, devices, and systems that are smaller than 100 nanometers (or about one-billionth of an inch). Some planned improvements include body armor that is soft and flexible until struck, when it becomes temporarily rigid and bulletproof. Nanotechnology may also provide a suit that senses its surroundings and changes coloration to camouflage a soldier. Medical nanomachines are planned that will be embedded in the soldier's suit. They will stop blood loss by making or becoming bandages, or perhaps by microscopically stitching wounds together.

Vision 2020 Future Force Warrior will also be extremely light. The current combat load of a U.S. infantry soldier is 92.5 pounds (42 kg). The Land Warrior system hopes to reduce this to about 80 pounds (36 kg), and the Vision 2020 Future Force Warrior is aiming to be only 45 pounds (20 kg).

As the name suggests, the plan is to deploy the Vision 2020 Future Force Warrior around 2020. The progress of nanotechnology will determine if this radical change in military equipment happens.

SUPPORT WEAPONS

Infantry support weapons provide every company with heavy firepower that is close by at all times. These weapons require crews to operate and are much more powerful than the personal weapons of the infantry soldier. There are three main weapons in this group: heavy machine guns, light mortars of about 60 mm, and antitank missiles. A new addition for the infantry of the future will be mechanical "mules" designed to haul extra ammunition, food, and power for the Future Force Warrior system.

HEAVY MACHINE GUNS

The most well-known infantry support weapon is the fearsome M2HB .50 caliber heavy machine gun. This weapon has a range of more than a mile (1,600 m) when mounted on the M3 tripod. Its bullets can crack engine blocks, pierce light armor, and penetrate the walls of buildings while still hitting with lethal force on the far side. This weapon has been in service since World War II, and its origins go back to World War I. It is a heavy piece of weaponry, weighing in at 128 pounds (58 kg), not including the weight of ammunition. The M2HB is a valuable weapon, but its weight makes it difficult for fewer than three men to carry it.

Two weapons will be replacing the M2HB: the XM-312 lightweight heavy machine gun and the XM-307 airbursting weapon system. The XM-307 is to be the eventual replacement. It will fire the same 25 mm grenades that the XM-320 launcher uses, but at 250 rounds per minute instead of one at a time. It will have the same effective range of the M2HB, but will be able to engage targets even more effectively by using both armor-piercing and high-explosive airbursting rounds. Its sights will enable it to function during the day and night. It will likely have a laser range finder to better control the grenade explosions. It can even be quickly and easily converted into a regular 12.7 mm machine gun for tasks in which that is more useful. All this will weigh about 50 pounds (23 kg), making it less than half the weight of the M2HB and easily carried by a two-man crew.

The XM-312 is essentially an XM-307 that is permanently in 12.7 mm configuration and does not have the sophisticated firing control of the XM-307. It will provide U.S. troops with a replacement for the M2HB while the XM-307 is being developed.

Seen here is a prototype of the XM-307 airbursting weapon system. The XM-307 can fire 250 grenades per minute and strike targets more than a mile (1.6 km) away. It is expected to be especially effective in taking out enemy soldiers who are hidden in foxholes or behind rocks or walls. It is being developed for the U.S. Army by General Dynamics, a weapons manufacturer based out of Falls Church, Virginia.

MORTARS

U.S. troops currently use the M-224 60 mm mortar. It weighs about 47 pounds (21 kg) and can lob twenty rounds per minute in a high arc out to 2 miles (3.2 km). Mortars provide invaluable support, giving each company the ability to quickly call down extra firepower on the enemy, lay down smoke for cover, or fire flares to light up the sky above the enemy.

Future improvements to the M-224 include devices to make it more effective, and new types of ammunition. The mortar ballistic computer will quickly make the complex calculations required for a mortar crew to hit distant and hidden targets.

Simple machines do this job now, but the mortar ballistic computer will do this even faster. New types of ammunition are being developed that will be fired in the general direction of a target, but will then follow a path set by a soldier who has pointed a laser at the target. This M-395 precision guided mortar ammunition is currently being developed for the larger 120 mm mortar. As the technology becomes smaller and more affordable, it is likely to appear in the smaller M-224.

ANTITANK WEAPONS

The current antitank weapon used by U.S. troops is the Javelin. It can destroy most armored vehicles and bunkers at a range of about 1.5 miles (2.4 km). The Javelin is a heat seeker. The soldier using it can "fire and forget," as opposed to earlier missiles like the M-47 Dragon that required the firer to remain exposed while guiding the missile to the target. As the Javelin nears an armored target, it arcs up into the air and then sharply descends, hitting the roof of the target and improving the chance of destruction. The Javelin entered service in 1996, but there are no plans for a new design. Gradual improvements in guidance and reliability can be expected over time. Like the M-240G, the Javelin looks to be serviceable for some years yet, so the army will spend its money on weapons upgrades elsewhere.

ROBOTS IN THE INFANTRY

The army is considering many different robots to provide support for the infantry. One is a mechanical "mule" that will carry

Pictured above is a testing version of a robotic tank called the Gladiator. The Gladiator will assist with many different types of missions, including scouting and reconnaissance, bunker destruction, and transportation of ammunition and supplies. The vehicle, which is roughly five feet (1.5 m) tall and five feet (1.5 m) long, will be operated by a remote-control unit with controls similar to those of a video game.

ammunition, food, batteries, and charging equipment for the Future Force Warrior electronics. It may even create drinking water through the use of hydrogen fuel cells.

Mine removal and demolition are other tasks likely to be taken over by machines. Robots may even be used to retrieve wounded soldiers and bring them to safety. While not yet practical, the army is planning to use robots for as many tasks as possible once the technology exists. The hope is that these machines will eventually greatly reduce risk to U.S. soldiers.

Robots such as the one pictured above have been used in U.S. operations in Afghanistan and Iraq to locate mines and explosives. These robots are also known as UGVs, or unmanned ground vehicles. UGVs, because they can take the place of human soldiers in dangerous situations, are expected to play an even bigger role in future warfare.

HEAVY SUPPORT

Related to infantry support weapons are indirect artillery and air strike capability. Soldiers in action, if they can precisely determine an enemy's position, often send that information back to an artillery unit or an aircraft unit. These units, known as heavy support, can drop devastating firepower on a target. In the future, gradual technological improvement of artillery and aircraft will allow support fire to be called in more quickly and with greater lethality.

The extended-range guided munition (ERGM) is a guided missile expected to become part of the navy's arsenal by 2007. The ERGM's main objective will be to provide precise firepower against enemy forces on land. The ERGM will be 5.1 feet (1.55 m) long and 110 pounds (50 kg). Raytheon, the company behind the Tomahawk cruise missile, the Patriot, and the AIM-9 Sidewinder, is manufacturing the ERGM.

An exciting future project in heavy support is the navy's planned Mark 34 Model 1 gun system. This will be a computerized 5-inch gun turret mounted on the Arleigh Burke–class destroyers. The gun will fire conventional shells, but will also fire extended-range guided munitions (ERGM). The ERGMs will use a guidance system based on global positioning system technology that will enable the hitting of targets more than 60 miles (97 km) inland. Currently, naval guns can only reach 13 miles (21 km) inland. There will even be a less expensive version of the ERGM with a range of 21 miles (34 km). This technology is likely to prove very useful when there isn't enough time to ship regular artillery and heavy support weapons to the mission site. This will give infantry of the future heavy support in all the coastal regions of the world.

NON-LINE-OF-SIGHT LAUNCH SYSTEM

The Non-Line-of-Sight Launch System (NLOS-LS) is a missile system that will likely appear with the Future Force Warrior in 2010. The NLOS-LS features two missiles: the loitering attack missile (LAM) and the precision attack missile (PAM). Both are launched from a container launch unit (CLU) on a helicopter or ground vehicle. LAMs will fly over the battlefield, transmitting the locations of

A precision attack missile is shot out of a container launch unit during a test by the Raytheon company, the missile's manufacturer. The precision attack missile is 7 inches (17.8 cm) in diameter and weighs about 120 pounds (54 kg). The container launch unit can hold up to fifteen missiles.

targets to a command center. The command center then decides whether to attack the target with a PAM (which is a guided missile), the LAM itself, or another type
of weapon.

LAMs and PAMs will share many components to keep costs low. The NLOS-LS will give commanders great awareness of the battlefield, as well as the ability to respond very quickly. Infantry of the future will be plugged into the information network. They will benefit from being able to mark targets and request missile strikes from the NLOS-LS vehicles and aircraft stationed near the battlefield.

INFORMATION MANAGEMENT

You may have heard the saying that "knowledge is power." This is certainly true concerning warfare. The U.S. military has long known the importance of accurate intelligence regarding troop positions and the enemy plans. The U.S. military calls this ability to outwit the enemy "information superiority." Information superiority, according to an official military document entitled *Joint Vision 2010*, is "the capability to collect, process, and disseminate an uninterrupted flow of information while exploiting or denying an adversary's ability to do the same." A major challenge of the U.S. military in the future will be to have information superiority over its adversaries.

Information superiority has become increasingly important over the years because of the changing nature of firepower on the battlefield. Weapons have progressed to the point that if a

A U.S. Army captain operates a computer at a communications center near Baghdad, Iraq. The captain is using a new command and control system called the Command Post of the Future. The system, which is designed to improve the flow of information from commander to soldier in the field, was tested for the first time in 2004.

target can be located, and it is within range, it can nearly always be destroyed. With the exception of deep underground bunkers, the United States has weapons that can defeat any protective measure likely to be encountered. These weapons are extremely precise. This is important to make sure the weapons strike only the target and not nearby buildings or homes.

Decreasing the damage done to people's homes and avoiding deaths of innocent people (known as collateral damage) is extremely important for modern and future warfare. International goodwill is maintained by protecting noncombatants through precise and careful use of force. The reduction of civilian casualties and property damage also eases tensions between civilians and troops in a combat zone. Most important, soldiers, commanders, and the leaders of nations have a moral responsibility to spare the lives of innocent civilians.

BATTLESPACE AWARENESS

Information superiority, when relating to a specific battle, is also known as battlespace awareness. The battlespace is the location where a battle is fought. This includes the land where the fight happens; the air above the battle; nearby bodies of water; and even outerspace, where satellites are monitoring troop movements.

As defined by the army, battlespace awareness is "the ability of joint force commanders and all force elements to understand the environment in which they operate and the adversaries they face." Battlespace awareness requires commanders and soldiers to be aware of the status of everything and everyone that can affect a particular battle. Ideally, this information should be provided to the soldier as it happens, which is known as "real time."

In the future, sensors and communications networking will significantly change the combat experience of infantry. Missions in which an infantry company is sent blindly into a building to drive an enemy out, leading to difficult and bloody fighting, will be a thing of the past. With battlespace awareness, a platoon will receive a detailed map of the layout of the building before it enters. Constant sensor surveillance of an enemy's location will be transmitted to the platoon. Once the enemy

M1A1 Abrams tanks are unloaded from trailers near the city of Mosul in northern Iraq on January 4, 2005. The M1A1, which entered service in 1985, is a powerful and well-protected tank, but it is also extremely heavy. Its weight of nearly 70 tons (63 tonnes) makes it difficult to transport via aircraft. Instead, the M1A1 is carried by much slower ground or sea transportation.

soldiers are located, clearing them out of the building becomes a much less dangerous fight.

Battlespace awareness is necessary to allow the U.S. military to lighten its combat forces and make them more mobile. The army plans to replace some of its heavy armored vehicles, such as the M1A1 tank, with lighter vehicles that are more easily transported. To survive without the protection that heavy armor provides, these lighter forces of the future will need to be aware of all enemy activity around them early enough to strike before they themselves are in danger. Battlespace awareness is the key to this early detection.

LAND WARRIOR AND BATTLESPACE AWARENESS

The Land Warrior system has a number of features that help with battlespace awareness. The thermal weapon sight previously discussed gives every infantry soldier the ability to sense the enemy in many conditions. It also allows the soldier to gather digital information. This collected information gets distributed over the communication network and turns every soldier into an additional set of eyes for other soldiers and commanders.

The Land Warrior system will use a wireless local area network (LAN) with a range of about half a mile (805 m) for intrasquad communications. This network handles short-range data and simple voice communications between squad members. Each soldier will have an individual subscriber identity module (SIM) card in his computer, which will identify the soldier and his unit, rank, and specialty. The SIM card will determine what kind of information a soldier can access from the computer system. Soldiers will be able to download text messages, maps, and satellite images. Commanders will be able to send information out over the system to select groups using the SIM card identification. For example, the commander might choose to send information about casualties to all the medics in Bravo Company.

Land Warrior squad leaders will have a commander's digital assistant (CDA) as a part of their computer gear. A version of the CDA is already in the field as a commercially manufactured

The U.S. Marine Corps has its own version of the commander's digital assistant named the dismounted data automated communications terminal, or D-DACT. This device allows marine unit leaders to send text messages to soldiers under their command, access maps, and link to the global positioning system for help with navigation.

personal digital assistant (PDA) that has been redesigned to survive on a battlefield. The CDA is equipped with a five-channel global positioning system connected to the SIM cards carried by the squad's soldiers. The location information is refreshed every thirty seconds, allowing the squad leader to know where each of his men is within thirty feet (nine m) of accuracy. For areas without GPS coverage, a pedometer built into each soldier's gear transmits his location over the intrasquad LAN.

Land Warrior greatly improves battlespace awareness at the squad level, keeping each soldier constantly updated with the locations of squadmates and enabling communication with them. Supplying power to the system is still something of a problem. Ten hours of power can be carried today, but the military hopes to increase that number. Although battlespace awareness provided by LW is still in the testing stage, it is the sort of technology that the U.S. military wishes to have throughout all echelons and branches of the service eventually.

FUTURE FORCE WARRIOR AND BATTLESPACE AWARENESS

The Future Force Warrior program is planned to build upon the technology of Land Warrior. Gradual advances will improve intrasquad communication, but the big changes will be in communication with soldiers and commanders from other squads. Soldiers will be able to share information with vehicles, aircraft, and other soldiers over a wide area. This ability to communicate directly with soldiers from other commands is very valuable. The high degree of communication will be available up through the highest levels of command, thus preventing problems, such as the ones experienced at the Battle of Mogadishu.

EXPERIMENTAL TECHNOLOGIES AND BATTLESPACE AWARENESS

Some experimental technologies promise to help infantry gather more information in the future. Micro air vehicles (MAVs) are tiny ultralight winged cameras the size of a paper airplane or smaller. They will act as disposable "eyes in the sky" devices to scout enemy-occupied buildings and positions. The MAVs will be functionally similar to the unmanned aerial vehicles (UAVs) currently used for long-range reconnaissance, but smaller in scale and in range. In

Micro aerial vehicles, such as this robotic fly, will likely see an increased role in future warfare. The military hopes to use the robotic fly, known as a micromechanical flying insect, for surveillance and reconnaissance of enemy troops and territory.

addition, nanotechnologists are exploring the viability of an intelligent "dust" of nanobots (microscopic robots) that can be scattered over a large area and transmit data about troop movements. There is even the possibility of turning that "dust" into a weapon that attaches to and attacks the delicate electronic components of enemy machines.

UNIT ORGANIZATION

For much of history, the infantry has functioned in a strictly hierarchical manner. Each soldier has soldiers of lower rank who answer to him, as well as those of higher rank whose orders he has to follow. In this type of system, soldiers must be trained to ignore personal desires in favor of what they are ordered to do. To make sure this happens, insubordination, which is disobedience to a superior officer, is harshly punished in the military.

CHAIN OF COMMAND

Chain of command is a system in which soldiers of various ranks are assigned to specific units, with specific people below and above them. For example, a lieutenant is generally not allowed to give commands to anyone from other units, even if they are of lesser rank. If assigned to platoon A

MILITARY UNITS

division　Unit under the command of a major general consisting of about 15,000 soldiers.

brigade　Unit under the command of a colonel consisting of 2,000 to 5,000 soldiers.

battalion　Unit under the command of a lieutenant colonel consisting of 500 to 1,200 soldiers.

company　Unit commanded by a captain or major consisting of about 120 soldiers.

platoon　Unit under the command of a lieutenant consisting of about 40 soldiers.

squad　Unit consisting of 8 to 14 soldiers.

of company C, he will give orders to the soldiers in platoon A. However, if he needs a squad from platoon B of company C, he will send the request to his commander in company C, who will then decide whether to order the lieutenant in charge of platoon B to send a squad over to help platoon A. The situation is much like a tree, where the lowest ranks are represented by the tips of the branches, and rank increases as one nears the trunk.

For commands and information to be transmitted between two branches (low-rank officers of separate units), they must go up the chain of command to a joint in the tree (a higher-ranked officer who has command of both the lower-ranked officers). At this point it can flow back down the chain of command to where it needs to go.

This system is useful because it ensures that every soldier knows his place in the structure of his unit. It also provides an easily understood and predictable flow of information. Finally, it prevents officers from accidentally giving contradictory orders to a unit, because all the orders pass though a single channel to get to the troops.

DRAWBACKS OF CURRENT MILITARY ORGANIZATION

Unfortunately, this system can be slow to react to new information. The Battle of Mogadishu serves as an example of this weakness. U.S. helicopters were hovering over the battle, trying to give directions to the troops on the ground so they could avoid roadblocks and ambushes set up by the Somalis. Unfortunately, the helicopter pilots had to give the information they gathered to their commanders, who gave it to the commanders of the ground troops, who radioed it to the men actually fighting their way out of the city. By the time the information got to the men on the ground, they had already run into the roadblocks and ambushes that the helicopters, which were right above them, were unable to warn them directly about. This drawback of current chain-of-command systems has led to a change in the way information will be shared in the U.S. military.

The previously discussed idea of battlespace awareness, combined with new communications capabilities like the ones seen in the Land Warrior and Future Force Warrior programs, are transforming the flow of information on the battlefield. Instead of resembling a tree, the flow of information will now resemble a net. Information will flow up and down and side to side in the command structure. This will allow for much more direct help to be given in situations like those at the Battle of Mogadishu.

In addition to the flow of information, the composition of units that make up the army and marines will also change. This is because heavy armored divisions are less necessary in today's warfare and in future warfare. Crisis management and peacekeeping missions, or limited wars against terrorists or guerrilla forces, cannot be responded to quickly enough by armored divisions, which can take months to deploy fully.

STRYKER BRIGADE COMBAT TEAMS

In recognition of this, the U.S. military began developing new brigade-sized units in 1999. These units can be deployed anywhere in the world in ninety-six hours. Currently, there are six of these brigades in operation. They will provide valuable experience for a more complete army transformation scheduled for 2008 to 2012.

These new brigades get most of their firepower from infantry, which is supported by light armored vehicles. The units were initially known as interim brigade combat teams. They have recently been renamed Stryker brigade combat

Three U.S. Army soldiers survey an area during a foot patrol in Mosul, Iraq, on December 10, 2004. The soldiers are part of the Twenty-fifth Infantry Division Stryker brigade combat team (SBCT). Visible in the background is a Stryker vehicle. There are six SBCTs as of 2005, each consisting of about 400 Stryker vehicles and 3,600 soldiers.

teams (SBCT), after the light armored vehicles that provide much of the brigades' support and transport. Some of the SBCTs were deployed to Iraq in 2004 to gain combat testing and experience.

There are about 3,600 people in an SBCT, but they are organized more like a miniature division than a typical infantry brigade. In addition to the Stryker-mounted infantry, the SBCT has support and field artillery battalions. It also has intelligence, signal, engineer, and antitank companies as part of its organization. Some brigades might have these additional units attached for special missions, but with the SBCT they train and function together as a team all the time.

Stryker armored vehicles patrol the streets of Mosul, Iraq, on October 4, 2004, during Operation Block Party. The vehicles are part of the Second Infantry Division Stryker brigade combat team. The armor surrounding the vehicles might not look very imposing, but it has been proven effective in stopping rocket propelled grenades and other weapons.

The SBCT's most innovative unit is a special battalion for reconnaissance, surveillance, and target acquisition (RSTA). This unit can maintain twenty-four-hour a day coverage of the enemy in a 30 by 30 mile (50 by 50 km) area.

STRYKER VEHICLES

The Stryker vehicles themselves are eight-wheeled armored cars of about nineteen tons (seventeen metric tons). They come in ten different varieties, such as infantry carrier, engineer vehicle, and medical evacuation. They share many parts to simplify supply and repair. The Stryker vehicles are expected to be integrated with the Land Warrior system beginning in 2006. Stryker vehicles will be issued equipment that will allow LW infantry to recharge batteries, communicate via voice intercom, and radio and exchange data with the Stryker crew. They will also provide improved communication for the LW squad with higher echelons, and allow troops to connect their computers to a central hub in order to synchronize data and intelligence information.

FUTURE FORCE WARRIOR ORGANIZATION

The Future Force Warrior program has not yet decided on any radically different organization for its soldiers. The military is waiting to learn from the experiences of the SBCTs and Land Warrior units before determining what organizational changes are needed. The only change planned at this time is a reduction in the size of infantry squads from nine to four men. Generally speaking, the FFW will probably see a similar trend throughout its organization. Increased precision firepower and better intelligence and communication will allow a few soldiers to do the work required by many soldiers today.

INFANTRY OF TOMORROW

The U.S. military realizes the need to adapt to the changing nature of warfare. Great effort is going into the Land Warrior and Future Force Warrior programs, which will be the foundation of tomorrow's infantry. There will also be larger organizational changes to provide the United States with an even more capable military. The infantry and the other armed forces are the United States' sword and shield. These new technologies and tactics will ensure that the infantry has everything it needs to protect the country effectively.

The infantryman has seen a gradual increase in status and importance over the past 100 years. In the next 100 years, he will become an ever more vital part of the armed forces.

A statue of a lone infantryman at the army base at Fort Dix, New Jersey, proclaims him to be "The Ultimate Weapon." Today, and continuing into the future, this proclamation could not be more true.

GLOSSARY

carbine A short-barreled, riflelike firearm.

collateral damage Unintended damage inflicted on people and property during military operations.

deploy To move into a battle-ready position.

destroyer A fast and heavily armed warship.

echelon One of the levels of command in an army.

fuse A device used to detonate a grenade, bomb, or other explosive when certain conditions are met.

hypothermia A condition in which a person's temperature drops dangerously below normal temperature.

incendiary An explosive device designed to start fires.

intelligence Information concerning the enemy.

modular Constructed in such a way to allow easy customization for different tasks.

mortar A short-barreled cannon used to send explosives in a high arc to a target.

reconnaissance The act of exploring territory to discover enemy troops and their positions.

strategic Related to the planning and directing of large military movements, such as a war. Having to do with the ultimate goal of a military action.

surveillance The act of keeping a close watch on enemy units or territory.

Taliban The political party that governed Afghanistan and sponsored the al-Qaeda terrorist network from 1996 to 2001.

tactics The plans devised to win small military movements, such as a battle.

FOR MORE INFORMATION

Federation of American Scientists
1717 K Street NW
Suite 209
Washington, DC 20036
(202) 546-3300
Web site: http://www.fas.org

Jane's Information Group
110 N. Royal Street
Suite 200
Alexandria, VA 22314
(800) 824-0768
Web site: http://www.janes.com

U.S. Army Natick Soldier Center
Future Force Warrior Liaison
Kansas Street
Natick, MA 01760
(508) 233-6977
Web site: http://www.natick.army.mil/soldier/wsit

U.S. Marine Corps
Headquarters Marine Corps
3000 Marine Corps
Pentagon 4B548
Washington, DC 20350-3000
(703) 614-4309
Web site: http://www.usmc.mil

Web Sites

Due to the changing nature of Internet links, the Rosen Publishing Group, Inc., has developed an online list of Web sites related to the subject of this book. This site is updated regularly. Please use this link to access the list:

http://www.rosenlinks.com/lfw/infu.

FOR FURTHER READING

Burnett, Betty. *Delta Force: Counterterrorism Unit of the U.S. Army*. New York, NY: Rosen Publishing Group, Inc., 2003.

English, John. *On Infantry*. Westport, CT: Praeger, 1994.

Hammes, Thomas. *The Sling and the Stone: On War in the 21st Century*. St. Paul, MN: Zenith Press, 2004.

Philip, Craig. *The World's Great Small Arms*. London, England: Brown Packaging Books, 2001.

Poolos, J. *Army Rangers: Surveillance and Reconnaissance for the U.S. Army*. New York, NY: Rosen Publishing Group, Inc., 2003.

Sun Tzu. *The Art of War*. New York, NY: Fine Communications, 2004.

Van Creveld, Martin. *Transformation of War*. New York, NY: Free Press, 1991.

Vizard, Frank, and Phil Scott. *21st Century Soldier: The Weaponry, Gear, and Technology in the New Century*. New York, NY: Time Inc., 2002.

BIBLIOGRAPHY

Barlelt, Eric. "Land Warrior." July 19, 2002. Retrieved March 11, 2005 (http://www.usma.edu/publicaffairs/PV/020719/Warrior.htm).

Berkowitz, Bruce. *The New Face of War: How War Will Be Fought in the 21st Century*. New York, NY: The Free Press, 2003.

Carter, Ashton B., and John P. White, eds. *Keeping the Edge: Managing Defense for the Future*. Cambridge, MA: MIT Press, 2001.

Cox, Matthew. "New and Improved Firepower: The Army's on the Hunt for Its Next Generation of Infantry Weapons—and the XM8 Is Not a Done Deal." March 21, 2005. Retrieved March 29, 2005 (http://www.armytimes.com/story.php?f=0-292925-904303.php).

Defense Update. "Future Combat Systems." 2004. Retrieved February 3, 2005 (http://www.defense-update.com/topics/topics-fcs.htm).

Director for Strategic Plans and Policy, J5: Strategy Division. *Joint Vision 2020*. Washington, DC: U.S. Government Printing Office, 2000.

Dunnigan, James F. *Digital Soldiers: The Evolution of High-Tech Weaponry and Tomorrow's Brave New Battlefield*. New York, NY: St. Martins' Press, 1996.

General Dynamics. "XM307," 2005. Retrieved March 1, 2005 (http://www.gdatp.com/products/lethality/xm307/xm307.htm).

GlobalSecurity.org. "U.S. Ground Warfare Systems," 2004. Retrieved March 10, 2005 (http://www.globalsecurity.org/military/systems/index.html).

Halter, Ed. "CGI Joe: How the Military and Private Tech Contractors Are Training a New Generation of Soldiers." *Village Voice*, February 9-15, 2005, pp. 38–39.

O'Hanlon, Michael. *Technological Change and the Future of Warfare*. Washington, DC: Brookings Institution Press, 2000.

1-115 Infantry. "Charlie Company," 2004. Retrieved March 1, 2005 (http://www.1-115inf.com/cco.php).

Shukman, David. *Tomorrow's War: The Threat of High-Technology Weapons*. New York, NY: Harcourt Brace & Company, 1996.

Steed, Brian. *Armed Conflict: The Lessons of Modern Warfare*. New York, NY: Ballantine, 2002.

United States Army. "About SBCT," November 7, 2003. Retrieved March 1, 2005 (http://www.lewis.army.mil/transformation/index.asp).

U.S. Army Natick Soldier Center. "Future Force Warrior," May 19, 2004. Retrieved February 2, 2005 (http://www.natick.army.mil/soldier/WSIT).

U.S. Department of Defense. *Joint Vision 2010: America's Military; Preparing for Tomorrow*. Washington, DC: U.S. Government Printing Office, 2000.

Vizard, Frank, and Phil Scott. *21st Century Soldier: The Weaponry, Gear, and Technology in the New Century*. New York, NY: Time Inc., 2002.

Williams, Cindy, ed. *Holding the Line: U.S. Defense Alternatives for the Early 21st Century*. Cambridge, MA: MIT Press, 2001.

INDEX

About the Author
Roderic D. Schmidt has been fascinated by military matters since seeing a tabletop war game as an impressionable ten year old. Over the years, his interest in the military became a more general interest in history, motivating him to get a BA in history at Trenton State College. He lives in New York City with his wife, Magdalena. He recommends the old *Squad Leader* wargame for those interested in infantry tactics and combat simulation.

Photo Credits
Cover U.S Army/FCS; cover (left corner) © Digital Vision/Getty Images; cover (top middle) © Photodisc Red/Getty Images; p. 6 and throughout Department of Defense photo by Petty Officer 2nd Class Katrina Beeler, U.S. Navy; pp. 7, 51 U.S. Army photo by Sgt. Jeremiah Johnson; p. 10 © Benjamin Lowy/Corbis; p. 13 © Daniel Morel/Reuters/Corbis; p. 16 photo courtesy of Program Executive Officer Soldier; pp. 17, 24 photo courtesy of U.S. Army; p. 19 Department of Defense photo; p. 20 DoD photo by Staff Sgt. Aaron Allmon; p. 26 © Bill Green/Frederick News Post/AP/ Wide World Photos; p. 28 Sarah Underhill, US Army Soldier Systems Center; p. 32 The Soldier/U.S. Army; p. 34 Systems Command/U.S. Marines; p. 35 © Wally Santana/AP/Wide World Photos; pp. 36, 37 © Raytheon Company; p. 40 © Jim MacMillan/ AP/Wide World Photos; p. 42 © AP/Wide World Photos; p. 44 Gunnery Sgt. Matt Hevezi/U.S. Marines; p. 46 © R. Fearing/ UC Berkeley; p. 52 DoD photo by Spc. John S. Gurtler, U.S. Army.

Designer: Evelyn Horovicz; Editor: Brian Belval